THE BLACK HAND

BY

ARTHUR B. REEVE

British Library Cataloguing-in-Publication Data
A catalogue record for this book is available from the
British Library

Arthur Benjamin Reeve

Arthur Benjamin Reeve was born on 15th October 1880 in New York, USA.

Reeve received his University education at Princeton and upon graduating enrolled at the New York Law School. However, his career was not destined to be in the field of Law. Between 1910 and 1918 he produced 82 short stories for Cosmopolitan magazine featuring his super-sleuth Professor Craig Kennedy. Kennedy is sometimes referred to as "The American Sherlock Holmes" due to his astounding ability at crime solving and his Watson-like sidekick Walter Jameson, a newspaper reporter. These characters featured in 18 novels, some of which were pseudo-novels stitched together from various short stories.

During this period he also began authoring screenplays, beginning with *The Exploits of Elaine* (1914). By the end of this decade his film career was at its peak with his name appearing on seven films, most of them serials and three of them starring Harry Houdini. Due to the film industry's migration to the west coast of America and Reeve's desire to remain in the east he produced less and less work for film. However, in 1927 he entered into a contract to write film scenarios for notorious millionaire-murderer, Harry K. Thaw, on the subject of fake spiritualists. The deal resulted in a lawsuit when Thaw refused to pay. In late 1928, Reeve declared bankruptcy.

Reeve continued to write detective stories for pulp magazines, but also covered many celebrated crime cases for various newspapers, including the murder of William Desmond Taylor, and the trial of Lindbergh baby kidnapper, Bruno Hauptmann. During the 1930s he became an anti-rackets crusader and produced a work of history on the subject titled *The Golden Age of Crime* (1931).

In 1932 he moved to Trenton to be near his alma mater. He died on 9th August 1936.

THE BLACK HAND

Kennedy and I had been dining rather late one evening at Luigi's, a little Italian restaurant on the lower West Side. We had known the place well in our student days, and had made a point of visiting it once a month since, in order to keep in practice in the fine art of gracefully handling long shreds of spaghetti. Therefore we did not think it strange when the proprietor himself stopped a moment at our table to greet us. Glancing furtively around at the other diners, mostly Italians, he suddenly leaned over and whispered to Kennedy:

"I have heard of your wonderful detective work, Professor. Could you give a little advice in the case of a friend of mine?"

"Surely, Luigi. What is the case?" asked Craig, leaning back in his chair.

Luigi glanced around again apprehensively and lowered his voice. "Not so loud, sir. When you pay your check, go out, walk around Washington Square, and come in at the private entrance. I'll be waiting in the hall. My friend is dining privately upstairs."

We lingered a while over our Chianti, then quietly paid the check and departed.

True to his word, Luigi was waiting for us in the dark hall. With a motion that indicated silence, he led us up the stairs to the second floor, and quickly opened a door into what seemed to be a fair-sized private dining-room. A man was pacing the floor nervously. On a table was some food, untouched. As the door opened I thought he started as if in fear, and I am sure his dark face blanched, if only for an instant. Imagine our surprise at seeing Gennaro, the great tenor, with whom merely to have a speaking acquaintance was to argue oneself famous.

"Oh, it is you, Luigi," he exclaimed in perfect English, rich and mellow. "And who are these gentlemen?"

Luigi merely replied, "Friends," in English also, and then dropped off into a voluble, low-toned explanation in Italian.

I could see, as we waited, that the same idea had flashed over Kennedy's mind as over my own. It was now three or four days since the papers had reported the strange kidnapping of Gennaro's five-year-old daughter Adelina, his only child, and the sending of a demand for ten thousand dollars ransom, signed, as usual, with the mystic Black Hand--a name to conjure with in blackmail and extortion.

As Signor Gennaro advanced toward us, after his short talk with Luigi, almost before the introductions were over, Kennedy anticipated him by saying: "I understand, Signor, before you ask me. I have read all about it in the papers.

You want someone to help you catch the criminals who are holding your little girl."

"No, no!" exclaimed Gennaro excitedly. "Not that. I want to get my daughter first. After that, catch them if you can--yes, I should like to have someone do it. But read this first and tell me what you think of it. How should I act to get my little Adelina back without harming a hair of her head?" The famous singer drew from a capacious pocketbook a dirty, crumpled, letter, scrawled on cheap paper.

Kennedy translated it quickly. It read:

Honourable sir: Your daughter is in safe hands. But, by the saints, if you give this letter to the police as you did the other, not only she but your family also, someone near to you, will suffer. We will not fail as we did Wednesday. If you want your daughter back, go yourself, alone and without telling a soul, to Enrico Albano's Saturday night at the twelfth hour. You must provide yourself with $10,000 in bills hidden in Saturday's Il Progresso Italiano. In the back room you will see a man sitting alone at a table. He will have a red flower on his coat. You are to say, "A fine opera is 'I Pagliacci.'" If he answers, "Not without Gennaro," lay the newspaper down on the table. He will pick it up, leaving his own, the Bolletino. On the third page you will find written the place where your daughter has been left waiting for you. Go immediately and get her. But, by the God, if you have so much as the shadow of the police near Enrico's your daughter will be sent to you in a box that night. Do not fear to come. We pledge our word to deal fairly if you deal fairly. This is a last warning. Lest you shall forget we will show one other sign of our power to-morrow. La MANO NERA.

The end of this ominous letter was gruesomely decorated with a skull and cross-bones, a rough drawing of a dagger thrust through a bleeding heart, a coffin, and, under all, a huge black hand. There was no doubt about the type of letter that it was. It was such as have of late years become increasingly common in all our large cities, baffling the best detectives.

"You have not showed this to the police, I presume?" asked Kennedy.

"Naturally not."

"Are you going Saturday night?"

"I am afraid to go and afraid to stay away," was the reply, and the voice of the fifty-thousand-dollars-a-season tenor was as human as that of a five-dollar-a-week father, for at bottom all men, high or low, are one.

"'We will not fail as we did Wednesday,'" reread Craig. "What does that mean?"

Gennaro fumbled in his pocketbook again, and at last drew forth a typewritten letter bearing the letter-head of the Leslie Laboratories, Incorporated.

"After I received the first threat," explained Gennaro, "my wife and I went from our apartments at the hotel to her father's, the banker Cesare, you know, who lives on Fifth Avenue. I gave the letter to the Italian Squad of the police. The next morning my father-in-law's butler noticed something peculiar about the milk. He barely touched some of it to his tongue, and he has been violently ill ever since. I at once sent the milk to the laboratory of my friend Doctor Leslie to have it analysed. This letter shows what the household escaped."

"My dear Gennaro," read Kennedy. "The milk submitted to us for examination on the 10th inst. has been carefully analysed, and I beg to hand you herewith the result:

Specific gravity 1.036 at 15 degrees Cent.
Water............................. 84.60 per cent
Casein............................. 3.49 " "
Albumin............................. .56 " "
Globulin............................. .32 " "
Lactose............................. 5.08 " "
Ash................................. .72 " "
Fat................................. 3.42 " "
Ricin............................. 1.19 " "

"Ricin is a new and little-known poison derived from the shell of the castor-oil bean. Professor Ehrlich states that one gram of the pure poison will kill 1,500,000 guinea

7

pigs. Ricin was lately isolated by Professor Robert, of Rostock, but is seldom found except in an impure state, though still very deadly. It surpasses strychnine, prussic acid, and other commonly known drugs. I congratulate you and yours on escaping and shall of course respect your wishes absolutely regarding keeping secret this attempt on your life. Believe me,

"Very sincerely yours,

"C. W. LESLIE."

As Kennedy handed the letter back, he remarked significantly: "I can see very readily why you don't care to have the police figure in your case. It has got quite beyond ordinary police methods."

"And to-morrow, too, they are going to give another sign of their power," groaned Gennaro, sinking into the chair before his untasted food.

"You say you have left your hotel?" inquired Kennedy.

"Yes. My wife insisted that we would be more safely guarded at the residence of her father, the banker. But we are afraid even there since the poison attempt. So I have come here secretly to Luigi, my old friend Luigi, who is preparing food for us, and in a few minutes one of Cesare's automobiles will be here, and I will take the food up to her-

-sparing no expense or trouble. She is heart-broken. It will kill her, Professor Kennedy, if anything happens to our little Adelina.

"Ah, sir, I am not poor myself. A month's salary at the opera-house, that is what they ask of me. Gladly would I give it, ten thousand dollars--all, if they asked it, of my contract with Herr Schleppencour, the director. But the police--bah!--they are all for catching the villains. What good will it do me if they catch them and my little Adelina is returned to me dead? It is all very well for the Anglo-Saxon to talk of justice and the law, but I am--what you call it?--an emotional Latin. I want my little daughter--and at any cost. Catch the villains afterward--yes. I will pay double then to catch them so that they cannot blackmail me again. Only first I want my daughter back."

"And your father-in-law?"

"My father-in-law, he has been among you long enough to be one of you. He has fought them. He has put up a sign in his banking-house, 'No money paid on threats.' But I say it is foolish. I do not know America as well as he, but I know this: the police never succeed--the ransom is paid without their knowledge, and they very often take the credit. I say, pay first, then I will swear a righteous vendetta--I will bring the dogs to justice with the money yet on them. Only show me how, show me how."

"First of all," replied Kennedy, "I want you to answer one question, truthfully, without reservation, as to a friend. I am your friend, believe me. Is there any person, a relative or acquaintance of yourself or your wife or your father-in-law, whom you even have reason to suspect of being capable of extorting money from you in this way? I needn't say that that is the experience of the district attorney's office in the large majority of cases of this so-called Black Hand."

"No," replied the tenor without hesitation: "I know that, and I have thought about it. No, I can think of no one. I know you Americans often speak of the Black Hand as a myth coined originally by a newspaper writer. Perhaps it has no organisation. But, Professor Kennedy, to me it is no myth. What if the real Black Hand is any gang of criminals who choose to use that convenient name to extort money? Is it the less real? My daughter is gone!"

"Exactly," agreed Kennedy. "It is not a theory that confronts you. It is a hard, cold fact. I understand that perfectly. What is the address of this Albano's?"

Luigi mentioned a number on Mulberry Street, and Kennedy made a note of it.

"It is a gambling saloon," explained Luigi. "Albano is a Neapolitan, a Camorrista, one of my countrymen of whom I am thoroughly ashamed, Professor Kennedy."

"Do you think this Albano had anything to do with the letter?"

Luigi shrugged his shoulders.

Just then a big limousine was heard outside. Luigi picked up a huge hamper that was placed in a corner of the room and, followed closely by Signor Gennaro, hurried down to it. As the tenor left us he grasped our hands in each of his.

"I have an idea in my mind," said Craig simply. "I will try to think it out in detail to-night. Where can I find you to-morrow?"

"Come to me at the opera-house in the afternoon, or if you want me sooner at Mr. Cesare's residence. Good night, and a thousand thanks to you, Professor Kennedy, and to you, also, Mr. Jameson. I trust you absolutely because Luigi trusts you."

We sat in the little dining-room until we heard the door of the limousine bang shut and the car shoot off with the rattle of the changing gears.

"One more question, Luigi," said Craig as the door opened again. "I have never been on that block in Mulberry Street where this Albano's is. Do you happen to know any of the shopkeepers on it or near it?"

"I have a cousin who has a drug-store on the corner below Albano's, on the same side of the street."

"Good! Do you think he would let me use his store for a few minutes Saturday night--of course without any risk to himself!"

"I think I could arrange it."

"Very well. Then to-morrow, say at nine in the morning, I will stop here, and we will all go over to see him. Good night, Luigi, and many, thanks for thinking of me in connection with this case. I've enjoyed Signor Gennaro's singing often enough at the opera to want to render him this service, and I'm only too glad to be able to be of service to all honest Italians; that is, if I succeed in carrying out a plan I have in mind."

A little before nine the following day Kennedy and I dropped into Luigi's again. Kennedy was carrying a suit-case which he had taken over from his laboratory to our rooms the night before. Luigi was waiting for us, and without losing a minute we sallied forth.

By means of the tortuous twists of streets in old Greenwich village we came out at last on Bleecker Street and began walking east amid the hurly-burly of races of lower New York. We had not quite reached Mulberry Street when our attention was attracted by a large crowd on one of the busy corners, held back by a cordon of police who were endeavouring to keep the people moving with that burly good nature which the six-foot Irish policeman displays toward the five-foot burden-bearers of southern and eastern Europe who throng New York.

Apparently, we saw, as we edged up into the front of the crowd, here was a building whose whole front had literally been torn off and wrecked. The thick plate-glass of the windows was smashed to a mass of greenish splinters on the sidewalk, while the windows of the upper floors and for several houses down the block in either street were likewise broken. Some thick iron bars which had formerly protected the windows were now bent and twisted. A huge hole yawned in the floor inside the doorway, and peering in we could see the desks and chairs a tangled mass of kindling.

"What's the matter?" I inquired of an officer near me, displaying my reporter's fire-line badge, more for its moral effect than in the hope of getting any real information in these days of enforced silence toward the press.

"Black Hand bomb," was the laconic reply.

"Whew!" I whistled. "Anyone hurt?"

"They don't usually kill anyone, do they?" asked the officer by way of reply to test my acquaintance with such things.

"No," I admitted. "They destroy more property than lives. But did they get anyone this time? This must have been a thoroughly overloaded bomb, I should judge by the looks of things."

"Came pretty close to it. The bank hadn't any more than opened when, bang! went this gaspipe-and-dynamite thing. Crowd collected before the smoke had fairly cleared. Man who owns the bank was hurt, but not badly. Now come, beat it down to headquarters if you want to find out any more.--

You'll find it printed on the pink slips--the 'squeal book'--by this time. 'Gainst the rules for me to talk," he added with a good-natured grin, then to the crowd: "G'wan, now. You're blockin' traffic. Keep movin'."

I turned to Craig and Luigi. Their eyes were riveted on the big gilt sign, half broken, and all askew overhead. It read:

CIRO DI CESARE & Co. BANKERS

NEW YORK, GENOA, NAPLES, ROME, PALERMO

"This is the reminder so that Gennaro and his father-in-law will not forget," I gasped.

"Yes," added Craig, pulling us away, "and Cesare himself is wounded, too. Perhaps that was for putting up the notice refusing to pay. Perhaps not. It's a queer case--they usually set the bombs off at night when no one is around. There must be more back of this than merely to scare Gennaro. It looks to me as if they were after Casare, too, first by poison, then by dynamite."

We shouldered our way out through the crowd and went on until we came to Mulberry Street, pulsing with life. Down we went past the little shops, dodging the children, and making way for women with huge bundles of sweatshop clothing accurately balanced on their heads or hugged up under their capacious capes. Here was just one little colony of the hundreds of thousands of Italians--a population larger than the Italian population of Rome--of whose life the rest of New York knew and cared nothing.

At last we came to Albano's little wine-shop, a dark, evil, malodorous place on the street level of a five-story, alleged "new-law" tenement. Without hesitation Kennedy entered, and we followed, acting the part of a slumming party. There were a few customers at this early hour, men out of employment and an inoffensive-looking lot, though of course they eyed us sharply. Albano himself proved to be a greasy, low-browed fellow who had a sort of cunning look. I could well imagine such a fellow spreading terror in the hearts of simple folk by merely pressing both temples with his thumbs and drawing his long bony fore-finger under his throat--the so-called Black Hand sign that has shut up many a witness in the middle of his testimony even in open court.

We pushed through to the low-ceilinged back room, which was empty, and sat down at a table. Over a bottle of Albano's famous California "red ink" we sat silently. Kennedy was making a mental note of the place. In the middle of the ceiling was a single gas-burner with a big reflector over, it. In the back wall of the room was a horizontal oblong window, barred, and with a sash that opened like a transom. The tables were dirty and the chairs rickety. The walls were bare and unfinished, with beams innocent of decoration. Altogether it was as unprepossessing a place as I had ever seen.

Apparently satisfied with his scrutiny, Kennedy got up to go, complimenting the proprietor on his wine. I could see that Kennedy had made up his mind as to his course of action.

"How sordid crime really is," he remarked as we walked on down the street. "Look at that place of Albano's. I defy even the police news reporter on the Star to find any glamour in that."

Our next stop was at the corner at the little store kept by the cousin of Luigi, who conducted us back of the partition where prescriptions were compounded, and found us chairs.

A hurried explanation from Luigi brought a cloud to the open face of the druggist, as if he hesitated to lay himself and his little fortune open to the blackmailers. Kennedy saw it and interrupted.

"All that I wish to do," he said, "is to put in a little instrument here and use it to-night for a few minutes. Indeed, there will be no risk to you, Vincenzo. Secrecy is what I desire, and no one will ever know about it."

Vincenzo was at length convinced, and Craig opened his suit-case. There was little in it except several coils of insulated wire; some tools, a couple of packages wrapped up, and a couple of pairs of overalls. In a moment Kennedy had donned overalls and was smearing dirt and grease over his face and hands. Under his direction I did the same.

Taking the bag of tools, the wire, and one of the small packages, we went out on the street and then up through the dark and ill-ventilated hall of the tenement. Half-way up a woman stopped us suspiciously.

"Telephone company," said Craig curtly. "Here's permission from the owner of the house to string wires across the roof."

He pulled an old letter out of his pocket, but as it was too dark to read even if the woman had cared to do so, we went on up as he had expected, unmolested. At last we came to the roof, where there were some children at play a couple of houses down from us.

Kennedy began by dropping two strands of wire down to the ground in the back yard behind Vincenzo's shop. Then he proceeded to lay two wires along the edge of the roof.

We had worked only a little while when the children began to collect. However, Kennedy kept right on until we reached the tenement next to that in which Albano's shop was.

"Walter," he whispered, "just get the children away for a minute now."

"Look here, you kids," I yelled, "some of you will fall off if you get so close to the edge of the roof. Keep back."

It had no effect. Apparently they looked not a bit frightened at the dizzy mass of clothes-lines below us.

"Say, is there a candy-store on this block?" I asked in desperation.

"Yes, sir," came the chorus.

"Who'll go down and get me a bottle of ginger ale?" I asked.

A chorus of voices and glittering eyes was the answer. They all would. I took a half-dollar from my pocket and gave it to the oldest.

"All right now, hustle along, and divide the change."

With the scamper of many feet they were gone, and we were alone. Kennedy had now reached Albano's, and as soon as the last head had disappeared below the scuttle of the roof he dropped two long strands down into the back yard, as he had done at Vincenzo's.

I started to go back, but he stopped me.

"Oh, that will never do," he said. "The kids will see that the wires end here. I must carry them on several houses farther as a blind and trust to luck that they don't see the wires leading down below."

We were several houses down, still putting up wires when the crowd came shouting back, sticky with cheap trust-made candy and black with East Side chocolate. We opened the ginger ale and forced ourselves to drink it so as to excite no suspicion, then a few minutes later descended the stairs of the tenement, coming out just above Albano's.

I was wondering how Kennedy was going to get into Albano's again without exciting suspicion. He solved it neatly.

"Now, Walter, do you think you could stand another dip into that red ink of Albano's!"

I said I might in the interests of science and justice--not otherwise.

"Well, your face is sufficiently dirty," he commented, "so that with the overalls you don't look very much as you did the first time you went in. I don't think they will recognise you. Do I look pretty good?"

"You look like a coal-heaver out of a job," I said. "I can scarcely restrain my admiration."

"All right. Then take this little glass bottle. Go into the back room and order something cheap, in keeping with your looks. Then when you are all alone break the bottle. It is full of gas drippings. Your nose will dictate what to do next. Just tell the proprietor you saw the gas company's wagon on the next block and come up here and tell me."

I entered. There was a sinister-looking man, with a sort of unscrupulous intelligence, writing at a table. As he wrote and puffed at his cigar, I noticed a scar on his face, a deep furrow running from the lobe of his ear to his mouth. That, I knew, was a brand set upon him by the Camorra. I sat and smoked and sipped slowly for several minutes, cursing him inwardly more for his presence than for his evident look of the "mala vita." At last he went out to ask the barkeeper for a stamp.

Quickly I tiptoed over to another corner of the room and ground the little bottle under my heel. Then I resumed my seat. The odour that pervaded the room was sickening.

The sinister-looking man with the scar came in again and sniffed. I sniffed. Then the proprietor came in and sniffed.

"Say," I said in the toughest voice I could assume, "you got a leak. Wait. I seen the gas company wagon on the next block when I came in. I'll get the man."

I dashed out and hurried up the street to the place where Kennedy was waiting impatiently. Rattling his tools, he followed me with apparent reluctance.

As he entered the wine-shop he snorted, after the manner of gas-men, "Where's de leak?"

"You find-a da leak," grunted Albano. "What-a you get-a you pay for? You want-a me do your work?"

"Well, half a dozen o' you wops get out o' here, that's all. D'youse all wanter be blown ter pieces wid dem pipes and cigarettes? Clear out," growled Kennedy.

They retreated precipitately, and Craig hastily opened his bag of tools.

"Quick, Walter, shut the door and hold it," exclaimed Craig, working rapidly. He unwrapped a little package and took out a round, flat disc-like thing of black vulcanised rubber. Jumping up on a table, he fixed it to the top of the reflector over the gas-jet.

"Can you see that from the floor, Walter?" he asked under his breath.

"No," I replied, "not even when I know it is there."

Then he attached a couple of wires to it and led them across the ceiling toward the window, concealing them carefully by sticking them in the shadow of a beam. At the window he quickly attached the wires to the two that were dangling down from the roof and shoved them around out of sight.

"We'll have to trust that no one sees them," he said. "That's the best I can do at such short notice. I never saw a room so bare as this, anyway. There isn't another place I could put that thing without its being seen."

We gathered up the broken glass of the gas drippings bottle, and I opened the door.

"It's all right, now," said Craig, sauntering out before the bar. "Only de next time you has anyt'ing de matter call de company up. I ain't supposed to do dis wit'out orders, see?"

A moment later I followed, glad to get out of the oppressive atmosphere, and joined him in the back of

Vincenzo's drug-store, where he was again at work. As there was no back window there, it was quite a job to lead the wires around the outside from the back yard and in at a side window. It was at last done, however, without exciting suspicion, and Kennedy attached them to an oblong box of weathered oak and a pair of specially constructed dry batteries.

"Now," said Craig, as we washed off the stains of work and stowed the overalls back in the suitcase, "that is done to my satisfaction. I can tell Gennaro to go ahead safely now and meet the Black-Handers."

From Vincenzo's we walked over toward Centre Street, where Kennedy and I left Luigi to return to his restaurant, with instructions to be at Vincenzo's at half-past eleven that night.

We turned into the new police headquarters and went down the long corridor to the Italian Bureau. Kennedy sent in his card to Lieutenant Giuseppe in charge, and we were quickly admitted. The lieutenant was a short, fullfaced, fleshy Italian, with lightish hair and eyes that were apparently dull, until you suddenly discovered that that was merely a cover to their really restless way of taking in everything and fixing the impressions on his mind, as if on a sensitive plate.

"I want to talk about the Gennaro case," began Craig. "I may add that I have been rather closely associated with Inspector O'Connor of the Central Office on a number of cases, so that I think we can trust each other. Would you mind telling me what you know about it if I promise you that I, too, have something to reveal?"

The lieutenant leaned back and watched Kennedy closely without seeming to do so. "When I was in Italy last year," he replied at length, "I did a good deal of work in tracing up some Camorra suspects. I had a tip about some of them to look up their records--I needn't say where it came from, but it was a good one. Much of the evidence against some of those fellows who are being tried at Viterbo was gathered by the Carabinieri as a result of hints that I was able to give them--clues that were furnished to me here in America from the source I speak of. I suppose there is really no need to conceal it, though. The original tip came from a certain banker here in New York."

"I can guess who it was," nodded Craig.

"Then, as you know, this banker is a fighter. He is the man who organised the White Hand--an organisation which is trying to rid the Italian population of the Black Hand. His society had a lot of evidence regarding former members of both the Camorra in Naples and the Mafia in Sicily, as well as the Black Hand gangs in New York, Chicago, and other cities. Well, Cesare, as you know, is Gennaro's father-in-law.

"While I was in Naples looking up the record of a certain criminal I heard of a peculiar murder committed some years ago. There was an honest old music master who apparently lived the quietest and most harmless of lives. But it became known that he was supported by Cesare and had received handsome presents of money from him. The old man was, as you may have guessed, the first music teacher of Gennaro, the man who discovered him. One might have been at a loss to see how he could have an enemy, but there was one who coveted his small fortune. One day he was stabbed and robbed. His murderer ran out into the street, crying out that the poor man had been killed. Naturally a crowd rushed up in a moment, for it was in the middle of the day. Before the injured man could make it understood who had struck him the assassin was down the street and lost in the maze of old Naples where he well knew the houses of his friends who would hide him. The man who is known to have committed that crime--Francesco Paoli--escaped to New York. We are looking for him to-day. He is a clever man, far above the average--son of a doctor in a town a few miles from Naples, went to the university, was expelled for some mad prank--in short, he was the black sheep of the family. Of course over here he is too high-born to work with his hands on a railroad or in a trench, and not educated enough to work at anything else. So he has been preying on his more industrious countrymen--a typical case of a man living by his wits with no visible means of support.

"Now I don't mind telling you in strict confidence," continued the lieutenant, "that it's my theory that old Cesare has seen Paoli here, knew he was wanted for that murder of the old music master, and gave me the tip to look up his record. At any rate Paoli disappeared right after I returned from Italy, and we haven't been able to locate him since. He must have found out in some way that the tip to look him up had been given by the White Hand. He had been a Camorrista, in Italy, and had many ways of getting information here in America."

He paused, and balanced a piece of cardboard in his hand.

"It is my theory of this case that if we could locate this Paoli we could solve the kidnapping of little Adelina Gennaro very quickly. That's his picture."

Kennedy and I bent over to look at it, and I started in surprise. It was my evil-looking friend with the scar on his cheek.

"Well," said Craig, quietly handing back the card, "whether or not he is the man, I know where we can catch the kidnappers to-night, Lieutenant."

It was Giuseppe's turn to show surprise now.

"With your assistance I'll get this man and the whole gang to-night," explained Craig, rapidly sketching over his plan and concealing just enough to make sure that no matter how anxious the lieutenant was to get the credit he could not spoil the affair by premature interference.

The final arrangement was that four of the best men of the squad were to hide in a vacant store across from Vincenzo's early in the evening, long before anyone was watching. The signal for them to appear was to be the extinguishing of the lights behind the coloured bottles in the druggist's window. A taxicab was to be kept waiting at headquarters at the same time with three other good men ready to start for a given address the moment the alarm was given over the telephone.

We found Gennaro awaiting us with the greatest anxiety at the opera-house. The bomb at Cesare's had been the last straw. Gennaro had already drawn from his bank ten crisp one-thousand-dollar bills, and already had a copy of Il Progresso in which he had hidden the money between the sheets.

"Mr. Kennedy," he said, "I am going to meet them to-night. They may kill me. See, I have provided myself with a pistol--I shall fight, too, if necessary for my little Adelina. But if it is only money they want, they shall have it."

"One thing I want to say," began Kennedy.

"No, no, no!" cried the tenor. "I will go--you shall not stop me."

"I don't wish to stop you," Craig reassured him. "But one thing--do exactly as I tell you, and I swear not a hair of the child's head will be injured and we will get the blackmailers, too."

"How?" eagerly asked Gennaro. "What do you want me to do?"

"All I want you to do is to go to Albano's at the appointed time. Sit down in the back room. Get into conversation with them, and, above all, Signor, as soon as you get the copy of the Bolletino turn to the third page, pretend not to be able to read the address. Ask the man to read it. Then repeat it after him. Pretend to be overjoyed. Offer to set up wine for the whole crowd. Just a few minutes, that is all I ask, and I will guarantee that you will be the happiest man in New York to-morrow."

Gennaro's eyes filled with tears as he grasped Kennedy's hand. "That is better than having the whole police force back of me," he said. "I shall never forget, never forget."

As we went out Kennedy remarked: "You can't blame them for keeping their troubles to themselves. Here we send a police officer over to Italy to look up the records of some of the worst suspects. He loses his life. Another takes his place. Then after he gets back he is set to work on the mere clerical routine of translating them. One of his associates is reduced in rank. And so what does it come to? Hundreds of records have become useless because the three years within which the criminals could be deported have elapsed with nothing done. Intelligent, isn't it? I believe it has been established that all but about fifty of seven hundred known Italian suspects are still at large, mostly in this city. And the rest of the Italian population is guarded from them by a squad of police in number scarcely one-thirtieth of the number of known criminals. No, it's our fault if the Black Hand thrives."

We had been standing on the corner of Broadway, waiting for a car.

"Now, Walter, don't forget. Meet me at the Bleecker Street station of the subway at eleven-thirty. I'm off to the university. I have some very important experiments with phosphorescent salts that I want to finish to-day."

"What has that to do with the case?" I asked, mystified.

"Nothing," replied Craig. "I didn't say it had. At eleven-thirty, don't forget. By George, though, that Paoli must be a clever one--think of his knowing about ricin. I only heard of it myself recently. Well, here's my car. Good-bye."

Craig swung aboard an Amsterdam Avenue car, leaving me to kill eight nervous hours of my weekly day of rest from the Star.

They passed at length, and at precisely the appointed time Kennedy and I met. With suppressed excitement, at least on my part, we walked over to Vincenzo's. At night this section of the city was indeed a black enigma. The lights in the shops where olive oil, fruit, and other things were sold, were winking out one by one; here and there strains of music floated out of wine-shops, and little groups lingered on corners conversing in animated sentences. We passed Albano's on the other side of the street, being careful not to look at it too closely, for several men were hanging idly about--pickets, apparently, with some secret code that would instantly have spread far and wide the news of any alarming action.

At the corner we crossed and looked in Vincenzo's window a moment, casting a furtive glance across the street at the dark empty store where the police must be hiding. Then we went in and casually sauntered back of the partition. Luigi was there already. There were several customers still in the store, however, and therefore we had to sit in silence while Vincenzo quickly finished a prescription and waited on the last one.

At last the doors were locked and the lights lowered, all except those in the windows which were to serve as signals.

"Ten minutes to twelve," said Kennedy, placing the oblong box on the table. "Gennaro will be going in soon. Let us try this machine now and see if it works. If the wires have been cut since we put them up this morning Gennaro will have to take his chances alone."

Kennedy reached over and with a light movement of his forefinger touched a switch.

Instantly a babel of voices filled the store, all talking at once, rapidly and loudly. Here and there we could distinguish a snatch of conversation, a word, a phrase, now and then even a whole sentence above the rest. There was the clink of glasses. I could hear the rattle of dice on a bare table, and an oath. A cork popped. Somebody scratched a match.

We sat bewildered, looking at Kennedy for an explanation.

"Imagine that you are sitting at a table in Albano's back room," was all he said. "This is what you would be hearing. This is my 'electric ear'--in other words the dictograph, used, I am told, by the Secret Service of the United States. Wait, in a moment you will hear Gennaro come in. Luigi and Vincenzo, translate what you hear. My knowledge of Italian is pretty rusty."

"Can they hear us?" whispered Luigi in an awe-struck whisper.

Craig laughed. "No, not yet. But I have only to touch this other switch, and I could produce an effect in that room that would rival the famous writing on Belshazzar's wall-- only it would be a voice from the wall instead of writing."

"They seem to be waiting for someone," said Vincenzo. "I heard somebody say: 'He will be here in a few minutes. Now get out.'"

The babel of voices seemed to calm down as men withdrew from the room. Only one or two were left.

"One of them says the child is all right. She has been left in the back yard," translated Luigi.

"What yard? Did he say?" asked Kennedy.

"No; they just speak of it as the 'yard,'" replied Luigi.

"Jameson, go outside in the store to the telephone booth and call up headquarters. Ask them if the automobile is ready, with the men in it."

I rang up, and after a moment the police central answered that everything was right.

"Then tell central to hold the line clear--we mustn't lose a moment. Jameson, you stay in the booth. Vincenzo, you pretend to be working around your window, but not in such a way as to attract attention, for they have men watching the street very carefully. What is it, Luigi?"

"Gennaro is coming. I just heard one of them say, 'Here he comes.'"

Even from the booth I could hear the dictograph repeating the conversation in the dingy, little back room of Albano's, down the street.

"He's ordering a bottle of red wine," murmured Luigi, dancing up and down with excitement.

Vincenzo was so nervous that he knocked a bottle down in the window, and I believe that my heartbeats were almost audible over the telephone which I was holding, for the police operator called me down for asking so many times if all was ready.

"There it is--the signal," cried Craig. "'A fine opera is "I Pagliacci."' Now listen for the answer."

A moment elapsed, then, "Not without Gennaro," came a gruff voice in Italian from the dictograph.

A silence ensued. It was tense.

"Wait, wait," said a voice which I recognised instantly as Gennaro's. "I cannot read this. What is this, 23 Prince Street?"

"No. 33. She has been left in the backyard," answered the voice.

"Jameson," called Craig, "tell them to drive straight to 33 Prince Street. They will find the girl in the back yard-- quick, before the Black-Handers have a chance to go back on their word."

I fairly shouted my orders to the police headquarters. "They're off," came back the answer, and I hung up the receiver.

"What was that?" Craig was asking of Luigi. "I didn't catch it. What did they say?"

"That other voice said to Gennaro, 'Sit down while I count this.'"

"Sh! he's talking again."

"If it is a penny less than ten thousand or I find a mark on the bills I'll call to Enrico, and your daughter will be spirited away again," translated Luigi.

"Now, Gennaro is talking," said Craig. "Good--he is gaining time. He is a trump. I can distinguish that all right. He's asking the gruff voiced fellow if he will have another bottle of wine. He says he will. Good. They must be at Prince Street now we'll give them a few minutes more, not too much, for word will be back to Albano's like wildfire, and they will get Gennaro after all. Ah, they are drinking again. What was that, Luigi? The money is all right, he says? Now, Vincenzo, out with the lights!"

A door banged open across the street, and four huge dark figures darted out in the direction of Albano's.

With his finger Kennedy pulled down the other switch and shouted: "Gennaro, this is Kennedy! To the street! Polizia! Polizia!"

A scuffle and a cry of surprise followed. A second voice, apparently from the bar, shouted, "Out with the lights, out with the lights!"

Bang! went a pistol, and another.

The dictograph, which had been all sound a moment before, was as mute as a cigar-box.

"What's the matter?" I asked Kennedy, as he rushed past me.

"They have shot out the lights. My receiving instrument is destroyed. Come on, Jameson; Vincenzo, stay back, if you don't want to appear in this."

A short figure rushed by me, faster even than I could go. It was the faithful, Luigi.

In front of Albano's an exciting fight was going on. Shots were being fired wildly in the darkness, and heads were popping out of tenement windows on all sides. As Kennedy and I flung ourselves into the crowd we caught a glimpse of Gennaro, with blood streaming from a cut on his shoulder, struggling with a policeman while Luigi vainly was trying to interpose himself between them. A man, held by another policeman, was urging the first officer on. "That's the man," he was crying. "That's the kidnapper. I caught him."

In a moment Kennedy was behind him. "Paoli, you lie. You are the kidnapper. Seize him--he has the money on him. That other is Gennaro himself."

The policeman released the tenor, and both of them seized Paoli. The others were beating at the door, which was being frantically barricaded inside.

Just then a taxicab came swinging up they street. Three men jumped out and added their strength to those who were battering down Albano's barricade.

Gennaro, with a cry, leaped into the taxicab. Over his shoulder I could see a tangled mass of dark brown curls, and a childish voice lisped "Why didn't you come for me, papa? The bad man told me if I waited in the yard you would come for me. But if I cried he said he would shoot me. And I waited, and waited--"

34

"There, there, Una; papa's going to take you straight home to mother."

A crash followed as the door yielded, and the famous Paoli gang was in the hands of the law.

www.ingramcontent.com/pod-product-compliance
Lightning Source LLC
Chambersburg PA
CBHW030136260626
47156CB00008B/2965